LARF

FOR THE GIRLS OF G406 — Ingrid, Kathryn,
Maddy, Maria, Marta, Meghan, Stephanie, Tara and Vera

Kids Can Press acknowledges the financial support of the Government of Ontario, through the Ontario Media Development Corporation's Ontario Book Initiative; the Ontario Arts Council; the Canada Council for the Arts; and the Government of Canada, through the CBF, for our publishing activity.

Published in Canada by
Kids Can Press Ltd.
25 Dockside Drive
Toronto, ON M5A 0B5

Published in the U.S. by
Kids Can Press Ltd.
2250 Military Road
Tonawanda, NY 14150

www.kidscanpress.com

The artwork in this book was rendered in vegetable-based watercolor, biodegradable ink, recycled paper collage and a dollop of Organic Sasquatch Detangler and Conditioning Shampoo. This book is vegetarian, vegan and sasquatch friendly.

The text is set in Giggles Wiggles BTN.

Edited by Tara Walker
Designed by Karen Powers

This book is smyth sewn casebound.

CM 12 0 9 8 7 6 5 4 3
Manufactured in Altona, Manitoba, Canada, in 8/2012 by Friesens Corporation

Library and Archives Canada Cataloguing in Publication

Spires, Ashley, 1978–
        Larf / written and illustrated by Ashley Spires.

For ages 3–7
ISBN 978-1-55453-701-3

I. Title.

PS8637.P57L37 2012   jC813'.6   C2011-904727-6

Kids Can Press is a **corus**™ Entertainment company

Written and Illustrated by
Ashley Spires

LARF

KIDS CAN PRESS

Have you ever felt like nobody knows you even exist? That's exactly how Larf feels. And he likes it that way.

Larf is a sasquatch. The only sasquatch, it seems.
He lives a quiet life in the woods with his bunny, Eric.

He was almost discovered once or twice. A hairy, seven-foot-tall, scarf-sporting manbeast is pretty hard to miss.

But luckily for him, people rarely believe in anything new and strange. And Larf is definitely strange.

Larf knows no one would ever leave him alone if they found out he was real.

The thought of all that attention makes him a bit sweaty.

Larf fills his days happily on his own, jogging ...

taking Eric for walks ...

and gardening.

Until one morning, he notices an odd article in the newspaper. It claims that a sasquatch is scheduled to make an appearance today in the nearby city of Hunderfitz.

How can that be? He's NOT PLANNING a TRIP to Hunderfitz. And even if he was, he certainly wouldn't be going on a Wednesday — it's laundry day!

Larf realizes this can only mean one thing: he is NOT the only sasquatch in the world!

This could change everything. Larf isn't sure he wants a change. But having another sasquatch around opens up so many possibilities ...

Teeter-tottering would no longer be impossible.

He could share hair grooming tips.

And his witty commentary on cheesy movies would no longer go to waste.
That settles it: Larf has to meet this other sasquatch!

Traveling to Hunderfitz is generally something that he avoids, but this is a once-in-a-lifetime opportunity. Besides, Larf is a master of camouflage. He is sure to go unnoticed.

BILLY, DON'T STARE.

WHAT *IS* THA

On the way, Larf starts to wonder what the other sasquatch will be like. If this guy is making appearances, then he could be a bit of a showboat. Larf isn't sure he wants to be around someone like that.

What if they don't get along?
What if the other sasquatch doesn't
like Larf?

What if he DOES like him and
wants to move in? What if he doesn't
pick up his laundry?

What if he eats meat?
What if he's allergic to Eric?

Or, worst yet, what if HE is a SHE?!
Larf really isn't ready to meet a girl.
He hasn't had a bath in ... ever!

By the time he arrives, Larf is having second thoughts. He really does enjoy being on his own.

ALL the activity, all the people and all the noise are making things worse. Larf can hardly see straight, let alone think straight, in all this hubbub!

SASQUATCH

THIS WAY

Does the other sasquatch actually like being around so many people? Will life with someone else always be this loud?

Suddenly, Larf spots the other sasquatch! But something doesn't seem quite right. Why are its eyeballs not moving? Is that a zipper down its belly? And since when could a sasquatch wear perfectly normal-sized running shoes?!

"You aren't a real sasquatch," Larf realizes aloud.

The other sasquatch removes its head. "Of course I'm not.

Sasquatches aren't real," the guy underneath replies.

Larf is disappointed, but at least he can return to his quiet life in the woods.

Then, while Larf is waiting for the bus back home,
a voice says, "Your bunny is super cute."

Larf looks up, and this time, what he sees seems exactly right.

It looks him right in the eyes and blinks!

It's covered in hair but has no zipper!

And its feet are **ENORMOUS!**

"My name is Shurl, and this is Patricia," the other sasquatch says, smiling. Like Larf, she had come to meet the "real sasquatch." Now, it seems, she has.

Larf invites her over for supper next Wednesday. (They are the only two of their kind in the whole world, after all. It's just the polite thing to do.) Shurl agrees. "But I should tell you, neither Patricia nor I eat meat."

Larf decides that just as soon as he gets home, he's going to have a bath. After he does his laundry, of course.